My Beautiful Birds

Suzanne Del Rizzo

pajamapress

First published in Canada and the United States in 2017

Text and illustration copyright © 2017 Suzanne Del Rizzo
This edition copyright © 2017 Pajama Press Inc.

10 9 8 7 6 5 4 3 2

www.pajamapress.ca   info@pajamapress.ca

 Canada Council   Conseil des arts    ONTARIO ARTS COUNCIL   Canadä
for the Arts   du Canada   CONSEIL DES ARTS DE L'ONTARIO
an Ontario government agency
un organisme du gouvernement de l'Ontario

The publisher gratefully acknowledges the support of the Canada Council for the Arts and the
Ontario Arts Council for its publishing program. We acknowledge the financial support of the
Government of Canada through the Canada Book Fund (CBF) for our publishing activities.

Library and Archives Canada Cataloguing in Publication

Del Rizzo, Suzanne, author, illustrator
        My beautiful birds / Suzanne Del Rizzo. ʺ First edition.
ISBN 978ʹ1ʹ77278ʹ010ʹ9 (hardback)
        I. Title.
PS8607.E4825384M93 2017   jC813'.6   C2016ʹ904791ʹ1

Original art created
with polymer clay
and acrylic

Publisher Cataloging‑in‑Publication Data (U.S.)

Names: Del Rizzo, Suzanne, author, illustrator.
Title: My Beautiful Birds / Suzanne Del Rizzo.
Description: Toronto, Ontario Canada : Pajama Press, 2016. | Summary: "Fleeing a home destroyed
in the Syrian Civil War, Sami worries about the pet pigeons he left behind. Even in the relative
safety of a refugee camp, the boy struggles to participate in daily activities, consumed by thoughts of
what he has lost. At last, when new birds in need of care enter his life, Sami begins the long road to
healing"— Provided by publisher.
Identifiers: ISBN 978ʹ1ʹ77278ʹ010ʹ9 (hardcover)
Subjects: LCSH: Refugees – Syria ʺ Juvenile fiction. | Refugee camps —Juvenile fiction. Birds –
Juvenile fiction. | BISAC: JUVENILE FICTION /Animals / Birds. | JUVENILE FICTION / Social
Themes / Homelessness & Poverty. | JUVENILE FICTION / People & Places / Middle East.
Classification: LCC PZ7.D457My |DDC [E] – dc23

Children's paintings created by: Isabelle Del Rizzo, Noah Del Rizzo, Tate Del Rizzo,
Connor Cormier and Evan Cormier

Cover and book design by Rebecca Bender

Manufactured by Friesens
Printed in Canada

E
452-1970

Pajama Press Inc.

181 Carlaw Ave. Suite 207 Toronto, Ontario Canada, M4M 2S1

Distributed in Canada by UTP Distribution
5201 Dufferin Street Toronto, Ontario Canada, M3H 5T8

Distributed in the U.S. by Ingram Publisher Services
1 Ingram Blvd. La Vergne, TN 37086, USA

To Lisa Dalrymple, Monica Kulling, and my amazing writer's group for your encouraging words, invaluable critiques, and friendship—your writing inspires my own.

THE GROUND RUMBLES beneath my slippers as I walk.
Father squeezes my hand. "It will be okay, Sami. Your birds
escaped too," he repeats. His voice sounds far away.
I squeeze back, hoping it will steady my wobbly legs.

Everyone I know is here. We are walking, one after the other.
"Just like follow-the-leader," says Father.

I remember filling my pigeons' food bowl, then—in a
flash—my neighborhood, and all that was home…gone.
And my beautiful birds?

I only looked back once when we were running to escape. In my mind I see them. Against the glowing Syrian skyline, dark flapping specks spiral upward. I know those wings. So steady. Strong.

"It will be okay, Sami. They escaped too."

We walk all night,
and all day,

and all night once more.

I count footsteps, never wanting to look up again.

As the sun peeks over the dunes to greet the new day, we arrive at the camp. Helpful hands welcome us in. We made it. We are safe.

A peaceful hush settles across the vast sea of shelters, but I can only hear loud booming in my head. I'm still scared. Mother wraps us up in rough blankets. We snuggle close and give in to sleep.

Days blur together in a gritty haze. All I have left are questions. What will we do? How long will we be here?

Father plants a garden. Neighbors open small shops.
Mother cooks *makdous* and flat bread.

But I am not hungry.

Sometimes the dry wind wafts soft music
through the camp. I shiver, remembering
the songs I would hum to my birds.
I wish they were here.

I wish it were like it used to be, just me and my
pigeons up on our rooftop with the wind and
the boundless sky.

Happy. Free.

Teachers open a school for the camp's children. They sing songs. They do math. I used to love to add and subtract.

At recess they play soccer. "Sami, come play!" calls my cousin. "You're great in net."

But I just watch...and wait.

One day we are given paints, paper, and brushes.
I try to paint my beautiful birds, knowing each
wispy feather by heart.

But the wisps turn to black.

Smoky black smears from edge to edge, swallowing everything underneath. I tear my painting piece by piece. Black paint stains my hands and my clothes. My stained heart is torn to pieces too.

Outside I run. I run to escape the blackness.

At the top of a dune, I stop in my tracks. "Is this my sky from home?"

The same rooftop clouds billow and swirl.

My sky waits like a loyal friend for me to remember.

I ask my sky to watch over my pigeons, wherever they are, to hide them in cloudy safety.

Now, when the smoky nightmares boom, I watch the clouds. Sometimes, fluffy cloud-pigeons take shape.
Spiraling.
Soaring.
Sharing the sky.

If I close my eyes, sometimes I can see my birds, and sometimes I daydream that I hear them.

"B-B-B-Birds?" I whisper.

But where...? How...? Whose?

   These are not my birds...but it doesn't matter.

   "You must be far from home too." Slowly, I stretch out my arms. Strong. The songs I tried to forget rush through me, as I hum softly. Steady. "Now you are safe."

A canary, a dove, a rose finch, and a pigeon.
Like feathered brushes they paint the sky with
promise and the hope of peace.
Plumes of yellow, rose,
shimmering turquoise, and white
all in harmony.

I gather the seeds and spilled lentils I find on the ground to feed my new feathered friends.

I trade *makdous* for paper and wool so they can build a cozy nest.

On bad days they know just what to say—*Chitter, chitter, cooo, cooo*—and what to do—nuzzle, nibble, cuddle...and when it is best just to be.

At school we make kites from discarded
bags, rope, and wood scraps that line the
pathways.

I paint feathers of yellow, rose, and
turquoise. Mixing my pigeon-gray paint,
I use just one dab of black.

Our kites zigzag and zoom in a game of tag.
The sunbeams flicker through the whirl of kites,
making the gritty sand sparkle.
Today is a good day.

From the river of fleeing villagers, new families trickle
through the gate.
 I spot a girl. Her eyes are brimming with tears for home.
 A shy smile warms my cheeks as I move quietly closer...
and gently hold out my hand.

"Hi. I'm Sami."

Author's note

In our world today, more families are displaced than ever before.
Sometimes, families are forced to flee their homes to escape war.
Right now this is happening in Syria, a country located in the
Middle East, along the eastern shore of the Mediterranean Sea. To
escape the bombing and dangers of a raging civil war that began in
2011, Syrians have fled on foot, often leaving everything behind, to
the nearby countries of Turkey, Lebanon, Iraq, Egypt, and Jordan.
Others have attempted the dangerous trip by boat across the
Mediterranean Sea from Turkey to Greece. Unable to find work
or buy a home in these new countries, they seek shelter wherever
they can, in makeshift housing in urban areas or refugee camps.
Jordan's Za'atari camp, constructed by the government of Jordan
in 2012, is run by the UN in partnership with many international
agencies as part of a massive emergency response to the Syrian
crisis. Today Za'atari houses close to 80,000 refugees, making it
the fourth largest city in Jordan. According to the UNHCR (The
United Nations Refugee Agency), as of July 2016, around 34,000
people per day are displaced due to conflict/war or mistreatment.
Approximately 65.3 million people are displaced around the world
today; 21.3 million of these are registered refugees. At this time, 6.5
million Syrians have been forced to flee their homes; half of those
displaced are children.

For more information and resources about the Syrian conflict, visit
pajamapress.ca/syrian_conflict_resources